This igloo book belongs to:

....

igloobooks

Published in 2015
by Igloo Books Ltd
Cottage Farm
Sywell
NN6 0BJ
www.igloobooks.com

SHE001 0715
2 4 6 8 10 9 7 5 3 1
ISBN 978-1-78440-215-0

Written by Jenny Woods

Printed and manufactured in China

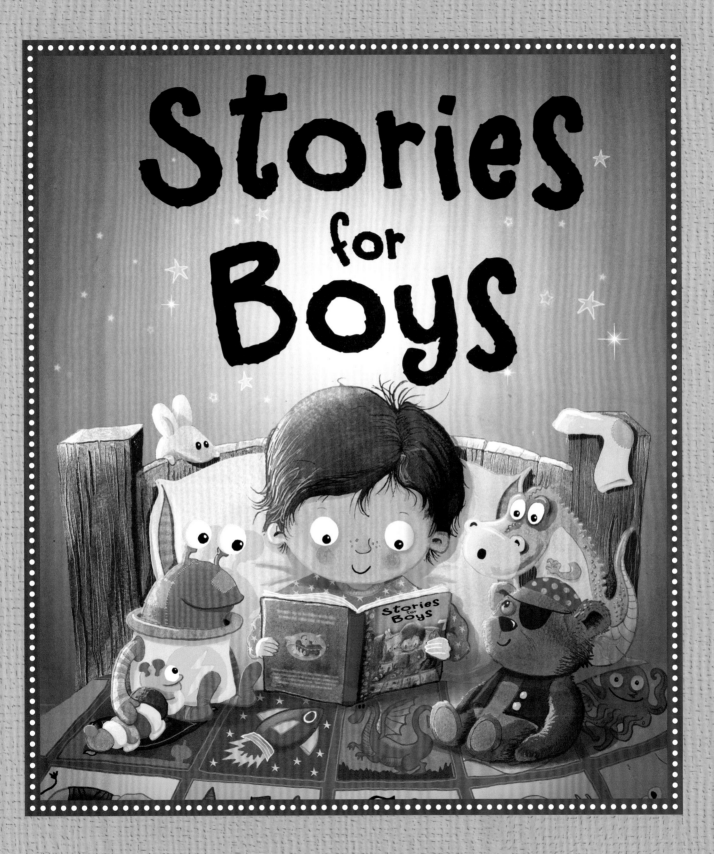

Stories for Boys

igloobooks

Contents

Dino Land

Billy was crazy about dinosaurs and wished more than anything that he could meet a real one. He couldn't believe it when Dad told him they were going to Dino Land for a day of dinosaur fun. When they arrived at the theme park, Billy couldn't wait to explore the whole place.

"Let's go to the Jurassic Jungle," said Billy, as they passed a huge, life-sized, model Triceratops. "Then, we can go and see the Lost Lake and the Prehistoric Swamp." So, Billy set off with Dad around Dino Land.
"Look at those Velociraptors," said Dad, pointing out the models to Billy.

Billy and Dad walked around Dino Land for hours looking at all the interesting things. Dad liked the Prehistoric Swamp most of all. "Look at those pretend dinosaur eggs," said Dad, but Billy didn't hear. He had found a bench to rest on and soon his eyelids began to feel heavy and they started to close. Before he knew it, Billy had drifted off to sleep.

Suddenly, Billy felt warm air on his face and he slowly opened his eyes. In front of him was a giant Brachiosaurus. "It's a real dinosaur!" gasped Billy. The Brachiosaurus nudged him gently with its nose. "You seem friendly," said Billy, "and I know you only eat plants!" So, Billy climbed onto its back and held on tight to its great, long neck.

The friendly Brachiosaurus stomped off slowly through the tropical jungle, taking Billy along for the ride. The dinosaur was so tall that Billy could touch the leaves on the tallest trees! He couldn't believe his eyes as they plodded past a Stegosaurus, a Diplodocus and a group of real Velociraptors.
Soon, they came to a lake and the Brachiosaurus stopped to have a drink.

"I wouldn't mind cooling off either," said Billy, who was starting to feel very warm in the tropical heat. "WHEEEEEE!" Billy slid down the long tail of his new Brachiosaurus friend and hopped off the end. He was just about to dip his toes in the lake, when he heard rustling from the nearby bushes.

"I wonder what's making that strange sound," thought Billy, tiptoeing over to take a look. As he peered into the undergrowth, a group of baby dinosaurs scampered out. They skipped in and out of the long grass and around the tropical plants. "That looks like fun," said Billy and he joined in the game.

12

Billy couldn't believe he was playing with real dinosaurs. He raced around the jungle with them, until they were all so tired that they fell into a heap on the ground. Suddenly, the ground started to shake and a loud noise rumbled through the jungle towards Billy. BOOM, BOOM, BOOM! "What's that?" he gasped.

Billy looked around, but his baby dinosaur friends had run away. ROOOAR! An enormous, angry-looking Tyrannosaurus rex crashed through the trees, chomping with its gigantic jaws. "Help!" cried Billy, as loud as he could, as the gigantic dinosaur stomped straight towards him. It was getting closer and closer and Billy held his hands over his eyes. Just then, he heard his name being called, "Billy! Billy!"

Billy opened his eyes to find Dad trying to wake him up. "Let's go and
see the T-rex," said Dad. "It really roars!"
"No, thanks," said Billy. "I've seen enough dinosaurs for one day."
Dad smiled. "Maybe you're right," he said. "Let's head to the gift shop instead."
Billy was relieved. "I had an amazing dinosaur adventure," he thought to
himself, "but I'm glad it was only a dream."

Alfie's Adventure

Alfie loved going for bike rides with his dad. Most of all, he liked riding through muddy puddles and making a great, big SPLASH! One day, as they were setting off for a long ride, Dad handed Alfie the map. "You can choose the route today, Alfie," he said. "Which way shall we go?"

"Let's go on the muddiest, bumpiest track!" cried Alfie. He couldn't wait to set off, over the hills and through the trees. So, Alfie stuffed the map into his backpack, next to the bag of special sweets he'd brought for the ride.

"Come on!" he called, putting on the backpack and pedalling down the track.

Dad and Alfie had a wonderful time as they rode through the countryside.
They whizzed over hills and zoomed through the fields.
"WHEEEEE!" cried Alfie, as he rode through a big, muddy puddle.
SQUELCH! "I'll race you through the woods!" he called to Dad,
ringing his bell. DING, DING!

Alfie made it through the woods first. "I win!" he said, catching his breath. Dad pulled up next to him, puffing and panting. "I think it's time we went home," he said. Dad and Alfie looked all around, but they didn't know which way to go. "Let's check the map," said Dad, so Alfie pulled off his backpack. "Oh, no!" he cried. "My backpack is open and the map is gone!"

Alfie passed the backpack to Dad. He rummaged around, then tipped out Alfie's water bottle, torch and an empty bag of sweets, but the map was nowhere to be found. "We're lost," said Alfie, looking worried.
"How will we ever find our way back to the car now?"
They had cycled up and down so many winding, muddy, twisting tracks that Alfie knew they would never remember the way back.

"Maybe the map fell out somewhere nearby," said Dad. Just as they started to look around, Alfie noticed something small and shiny on the ground.
"It's one of my sweets!" he cried, excitedly. "I brought a whole bag with me in my backpack. They must have all fallen out, just like the map."

"It looks like you've left a trail for us to follow," said Dad, laughing.
"Here's another sweet," he said, pointing up the track, "and another."
So, Dad and Alfie set off, back through the woods, through the fields and over
the hills. They went wherever the trail of sweets took them, until suddenly,
they looked up and saw the car. "We made it!" they yelled, excitedly.

"I wonder where the map got to in the end," said Dad.
Then, Alfie looked down and saw the map. It had fallen straight into a muddy puddle on the ground.
"Sorry, Dad," said Alfie, picking it up. "I didn't mean to get us lost."
"Don't worry," said Dad, kindly, "but I think I'll hang on to the map on our next biking adventure!"

Super Saver

It was the final of the Golden Boots Cup and the Red Roosters were playing the Blue Bears. The crowd was ready and the players were warming up. Sam was a reserve for the Reds and he couldn't wait to cheer on his team, even if it was only from the bench. "Come on, Red Roosters!" he yelled.

TOOT, TOOT! The Blues kicked off. "Over here!" cried one player.
"I'm free!" called another, as they passed the ball from player to player.
"SHOOT!" The star striker for the Blue Bears kicked the ball straight into the
back of the net and the crowd clapped and cheered. "WOO-HOO!"

Just then, Sam noticed some of his teammates gathered round their goalkeeper, Ned. "Ouch!" wailed Ned, sitting on the floor and clutching his ankle. Sam watched his teammates help Ned off the pitch, limping. "It looks like you'll have to take my place," said Ned, passing him. Sam could hardly believe it. He was going to play in the most important match of the season!

Sam's tummy felt like it was full of butterflies as the whistle went, TOOT! The Blue Bears' striker came charging at the goal and launched the ball into the air with one great big kick. WHOOSH! Before he knew it, Sam had leapt up and knocked the ball away.

Sam had saved his first goal of the match! "I can't believe it," whispered Sam to himself, but there was no time to celebrate. One of the Blues was already weaving through the Reds' defence, towards Sam. Their player took a shot, but Sam couldn't head the ball away in time. "Don't worry, you'll save the next one, Sam!" his team called.

Now, it was the Red's turn to head towards the goal. Their striker had tackled one of the Blues and taken the ball. Sam watched from the goal as the striker charged down the field. "Come on, Reds!" called Sam, as they scored their first goal.

The crowd whooped and yelped even louder as the Reds scored again. They were drawing with the Blue Bears!

Just then, the Blues tried to shoot from the halfway line. "That's an easy one to save," said Sam, smiling and kicking the ball out of the way.

The Red Roosters only needed one more goal to beat the Blue Bears and Sam was beaming with pride. "We're sure to win now!" he thought. Then, Sam saw the Blues approaching the penalty box and soon, the ball was in the air. It soared up over his head. "I'll never reach it!" he cried. Leaping up and stretching out his arms, he just managed to catch the ball with his fingertips. "YES!" cried the Reds.

Sam kicked the ball out to midfield where his teammates were waiting.
They dribbled the ball back down the pitch, passing backwards and forwards.
Then, a hush fell over the crowd as the ball soared over the Blue goalie's head
and into the net. The Red Roosters had won, just as the whistle blew!
They had all played so well, but the real star of the match was Sam.
"You really saved the day!" his teammates cheered.

The Red Rocket

Tommy had spent ages building a shiny, red rocket and he couldn't wait to play with it. "I'm going to have a brilliant space adventure," he said. "WHIZZ, ZOOM!" Tommy worked hard all day to finish his rocket, but it didn't look quite right. "I've glued the nose on wonky," said Tommy, "and it's already dry. My rocket will never fly properly now!"

Tommy was very disappointed and he ran downstairs to tell Dad. "My rocket is broken!" he cried. "Now I can't go on a space adventure!"

"Don't worry, I've got something that will really cheer you up," said Dad.

"We're going to Space World! The tickets are extra special, too."

"Wow, thanks Dad!" cried Tommy, bouncing up and down with excitement.

Dad knew how much Tommy loved rockets, so a trip to Space World was the perfect treat. When they arrived, two people in alien costumes greeted them. "Put these on," said the purple alien, handing them each a helmet and a spacesuit. "Because your Space World tickets are special, today you're going to be just like a real astronaut!" Tommy gasped. He couldn't believe they were going to have a real space adventure after all.

When they looked around, the sky was full of twinkling stars and there were amazing space rides everywhere. There was a giant planet with rings around it. "This looks like a great helter-skelter ride," said Tommy. "WHEEEE!"
Next, he jumped on a bouncy space castle and played crazy golf in a moon crater. Suddenly, Tommy heard a crackly voice overhead. "This is Mission Control," it said. "Tommy is to report to the Red Rocket."

Tommy and Dad climbed into the Red Rocket, just in time for the countdown. 3...2...1... BLAST OFF! They launched into space with a WHOOSH and a BANG. "Wow!" cried Tommy, as he saw stars and planets whizz by. "Ooo," he whispered, when a fiery comet flew past. Then, Tommy's insides jiggled and jumped, as they bumped and bounced through a rocky meteor shower. "Hold on tight," said Dad.

Soon, the Red Rocket returned to Earth with a BUMP and the doors opened with a SWISH. "Phew!" puffed Dad, stepping out of the rocket. "Did you enjoy your space adventure?" Tommy nodded. He had felt just like a real astronaut. "When we get home, I'm going to fix my rocket," said Tommy, "and this time, it's going to really fly!"

Jamie's Jokes

Jamie loved playing jokes on his family. When his sister, Amy, sat down on the sofa, he would creep up behind her, take a deep breath and blow a raspberry, as loud as he could. Amy would jump when she heard the noise, until there was chuckling from behind the sofa. "Jamie!" she would cry, angrily, as he snuck out of the room.

Jamie loved to play tricks on his dad, too. When Dad was busy in the garden, Jamie found a big pile of leaves and hid under it. As soon as Dad walked past, Jamie leapt out of the leaves and shouted, "BOO!"
Dad jumped in surprise and stumbled backwards. "Jamie!" cried Dad, as his naughty son scampered back inside.

One day, Jamie hid a spider in Mum's shoe. When Mum saw it, she gave a spine-tingling scream. "AARGHHH!"
Then, Mum realised it was only a plastic spider and sighed.
"Jamie's playing jokes again," she said, with a frown. "I think it's time he learned a lesson!"

Mum, Dad and Amy thought hard about what to do. "Why don't we play a trick on Jamie?" suggested Amy. "Then, he will find out exactly what it's like." Everyone nodded in agreement and started to think about how to get their own back for all the tricks Jamie had played on them. Soon, Jamie's family had the perfect plan.

The next morning, Mum, Dad and Amy waited at the bottom of the stairs. Mum had been to the joke shop and bought a special, trick plant pot. When Jamie finally appeared, Mum waited for him to take a sniff of the flowers in the pot. "Don't they smell lovely?" she asked him.

WHOOSH! As soon as Jamie leaned down to smell Mum's flowers, a squirt of water shot out and went all over him. "You tricked me!" cried Jamie, wiping the drips off his nose. Just then, Dad and Amy appeared. They took one look at Jamie who was dripping wet and scowling and they burst out laughing.

Mum chuckled...   ... Amy giggled...

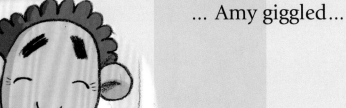

... and Dad held his
belly as he laughed
out loud.

Eventually, even Jamie couldn't help laughing, too. "We thought you should
find out what it's like to have a joke played on you," explained Mum.
She smiled and handed Jamie a towel.
"So, we decided to teach you a lesson," added Dad.
"You looked so funny!" cried Amy, as everyone started chuckling again.

"That was a brilliant trick," admitted Jamie, "but I suppose I can see why you're fed up with all my pranks."
He dried himself off and they all sat down to have breakfast together.
"I promise I won't play jokes on you anymore," said Jamie, as he tucked into his bowl of cereal. Then he gave a big, cheeky grin. "Well, for a day or two!"

Rock Star

Ben loved music and he had always wanted to be a rock star. "WOO-HOO! YEAH!" shouted Ben, as he strummed a pretend guitar. He turned up the radio and sang along to the song, closing his eyes and rocking to the beat. Then, Ben looked down at his clothes. "I'll never be a rock star looking like this," he said.

So, Ben found a rock star t-shirt and spiked up his hair with Dad's hair gel. "Every rock star needs some rock star sunglasses," he said, rummaging in his drawers to find some cool shades. Ben looked in the mirror and struck a cool, rock star pose. "Now I'm ready to rock!" he shouted.

Ben searched all over the house for an instrument to play, but all he could find was his sister's recorder. It was pink and sparkly and not at all right for a rock star. "I suppose this will have to do," said Ben. He closed his eyes, took a deep breath and puffed up his cheeks. Then, Ben blew as hard as he could into the recorder. It made a terrible noise. SQUEAK, SQUEAK!

"Maybe the recorder isn't right for a rock star," said Ben. So, he dashed
downstairs to perform for his dad, instead. Ben sang so loudly that
suddenly, Mum called to Dad from the kitchen. "Is there a cat meowing
outside?" she asked. Dad chuckled to himself. "I think you might have
forgotten the words, Ben," he said, kindly.

Ben felt fed up as he trudged into the kitchen. "I'll never be a rock star," he sighed. "Don't give up," said Mum. "It takes time to become a star." Just then, Ben's baby brother started hitting the side of his bowl with a spoon. DUM! DI-DI! DUM-DUM! The sound gave Ben an idea.

"That makes a great beat," said Ben. "I think I know how I can be a rock star after all." Ben collected pots, pans and wooden spoons from around the kitchen and before long, he had arranged them on the table to make his very own drum kit.

Ben practised all afternoon, while his family listened to the loud noises he was making. BANG! CRASH! "What a terrible noise!" cried Mum, putting her hands over her ears.

"I hope the neighbours don't complain!" yelled Dad. Then, they smiled at one another and decided it would be much more fun to join in.

So, Ben's family had fun making lots of music together, all evening.
Ben's sister sang into her hairbrush, Mum and Dad played their pretend
guitars and Ben and his baby brother played the drums.
By the end of the day, Ben decided that he didn't want to be a rock
star on his own anymore. "It's much more fun being in a band!" he said.

Making Friends

Scott had just moved house with his family and it felt strange being in a new place. He missed his old room, but most of all, Scott missed his friends. He looked out of the window at the skate park across the road. He loved skateboarding with his friends and it made him miss them even more. Just then, Dad poked his head around the door.

54

"Why don't we go and explore?" suggested Dad, in a cheerful voice. "We can even go to the skate park if you like."

"Yes, please," said Scott, excitedly, but then, he started to feel nervous.

"What if the people there don't like me?" he asked Dad.

"Don't worry," said Dad. "You'll make new friends in no time."

Dad helped Scott put on his helmet and pads. Then, Scott grabbed his skateboard and they headed off to the park. When they got there, it was full of children on skateboards and roller skates. There were ramps and slopes everywhere and everyone looked like they were having fun.

"It's amazing!" cried Scott, looking around. He couldn't wait to join in.

Soon, three boys whooshed over on their skateboards. "That's a cool board,"
said one of them to Scott. "Do you want to come and play with us?"
Suddenly, Scott felt really shy, but Dad whispered in his ear.
"Go on," said Dad, kindly. So, Scott picked up his skateboard and joined
the boys. "I'm Matt," said one, "and this is Aaron and Simon."

Scott wobbled on his skateboard at first as he followed the boys to the ramps, but soon, they were zigzagging around the park together. "You've got to try this half-pipe," said Simon. "It's brilliant!" He whooshed down the slope and zoomed up the other side. "WHEEEE!" Scott went next and his nerves soon disappeared as he whizzed down the ramp.

"Do you want to see my new trick?" asked Aaron, after they'd zoomed down another ramp, one after the other. The boys nodded, so Aaron soared down the slope and whooshed high up into the air, bending his knees and holding his board. "That's amazing!" cried Matt.

"I wish I knew some cool tricks," said Simon, with a sigh.

"I know a good one," said Scott, but suddenly, he felt nervous. "What if I fall over and they laugh at me?" he thought.

Then, Scott gathered up all his courage and picked up his board. He whizzed down the slope, flipped his board over and landed on it again. The boys all whooped and cheered.

"That was brilliant," said Aaron. "Please show us how to do that!"

"Sorry boys, it's time for Scott to go home," said Dad, strolling over. So, Scott waved goodbye to his new friends and promised to teach them his trick the next time he came to the park.

"It was fun making new friends," said Scott, as they walked back to their new home together.

Tree House Trouble

Harry couldn't wait for his friends Jake, Zack and Josh to come round and play in his new tree house. It was the perfect place to hang out in, but that morning, Harry got a nasty surprise. Someone had been in the tree house and made a terrible mess! Just then, Harry's friends climbed up after him.

"Who's pulled all the pictures off the walls?" asked Jake, sounding puzzled.
"Someone's eaten all our snacks," added Zack, spotting the crumbs and empty wrappers all over the floor.
"There are toys everywhere," said Josh, looking around.
"It's the mystery of the messy tree house," said Harry, who loved detective stories. "Let's investigate."

The boys got straight to work, searching for clues. It was hard to find anything in all the mess, but before long, Harry spotted something.

"There's some brown fur on this cushion," he said. "I think it's from my sister Rosie's teddy bear."

"Let's go and find out," said Jake.

The boys found Rosie playing with her dolls. "I didn't do it," insisted Rosie, when the boys told her about their messy tree house. "I'm scared of heights, so it couldn't possibly have been me!"

"She's right," said Harry, remembering how Rosie was always too scared to go on the climbing frame at the park. So, they all went to look for more clues.

Harry and his friends searched for anything that would help them solve the mystery of the messy tree house. Then, Zack discovered some empty hazelnut shells under the table. "My dad likes nuts," said Harry, "but I don't think he would have messed up the tree house. He was the one who built it for me!" "Let's go and ask him," said Josh.

Harry's dad was busy washing his car when the boys found him. When they asked if it was him who had been in the tree house, Harry's dad laughed out loud. "I'm much too big to fit through that tiny door," he pointed out. "I think I know how you can find out who did do it, though."

The boys followed Dad into the garden and hid under lots of leaves. "Keep a very close watch on the tree house," said Dad. "Then, keep quiet and wait for whoever did it to come back." After a while, the boys heard a noise. RUSTLE, RUSTLE! "I think we've found the culprits," whispered Jake, as two squirrels scampered into the tree house.

Harry and his friends told Dad all about the squirrels. "Why don't we make them a place of their own?" suggested Dad.

So, the boys filled a box full of nuts and left it in the garden. It was the perfect place for squirrels! "I think we'll have the tree house to ourselves from now on," said Harry.

69

Monster Mayhem

George was going to a monster party and he couldn't wait to dress up in a scary costume. "I'm going to be the scariest monster at the whole party," said George, as he dashed upstairs to get ready. George rummaged through the dressing-up box, but he didn't think that a cowboy hat, a fairy wand or anything else he found was very scary at all.

"These things won't make a scary costume," said George. "I'll just look silly.
What am I going to wear now?" Just then, Mum came in and noticed George
looking disappointed. She smiled and put her arm around him.
"Don't worry," she said, "we'll make you your very own monster
costume instead." George brightened up and they got straight to work.

Mum helped George find all sorts of things for his costume from her craft box. "This furry fabric will make a great monster suit," said George, picking out some material. "Every monster needs a gruesome, scary face!" he added, sloshing bright green paint over a cardboard mask.
By the time they had finished, George couldn't wait to wear his new costume.

George decided to practise roaring like a monster for the party. "ROAR!"
Then, he tried making scary monster poses. He put his hands above his head
and made a low, growling sound. "GRRRR!"
George looked brilliant as a monster, but he still felt worried. "What if
everyone laughs at me?" he thought to himself.

73

When George arrived at the monster party, he was still feeling nervous about his costume. He knocked on the door and it creaked open, slowly. Standing in the doorway was a ghost, a skeleton and a vampire. They were George's friends, all dressed up in their scary outfits. As soon as they saw him, they all let out a spine-tingling scream. "AAAAARGH!"

George took off his mask and giggled. "Oh, it's you, George," said his friends. "You gave us such a fright! I wish our costumes were as scary as yours." George was so pleased that his costume looked super-scary. He went inside with his friends and couldn't wait to enjoy the rest of the party.

Now that George was one of the scariest monsters at the party, he didn't feel nervous at all. He was even given a special prize for wearing the best costume. He felt so proud that he took a deep breath and gave his very loudest, "ROOOOOAAR!"

For the rest of the party, George had a great time playing spooky party games. He liked Hide-and-Shriek the best! He leapt out from behind doors to make his friends jump and even showed them how to do a monster dance. "I love dressing up as a scary monster," said George. "I think I'll make all of my own party costumes from now on."

Racing Wheels

It was nearly time for the big go-kart race and Jack was desperate to take part. There was just one problem. Jack didn't have a go-kart. "I'd love to zoom round the track in a super-fast go-kart," said Jack, sighing.

"Let's make our own," said Dad. "I've got lots of old parts in the shed."

"That's a brilliant idea," said Jack. He helped Dad rummage around to find everything they needed. "These wooden boxes are just right," said Jack, "and the wheels from the old pram are perfect!"

Dad showed Jack how to fix all the parts together. Then, they added a steering wheel and some brakes. Jack even found himself a horn. He squeezed it and made Dad jump. HONK, HONK!

Jack and his dad worked on the go-kart all day long. "We're like a real racing team," said Jack, passing Dad another part. To finish it off, they found an old cushion for the seat and two torches to make headlights.

Before long, Jack's new go-kart was nearly ready to race.

"Now, we just need to paint it," said Dad, handing Jack a box of paint pots.

Jack picked out a pot of bright red paint and sloshed it all over the go-kart. Soon, it looked as sleek and shiny as a real racing car and Jack couldn't wait to race it. "It looks amazing!" cried Jack, jumping up and down with excitement. "I'll have the best go-kart in the whole race."

On the day of the big race, Jack's tummy was fluttering with excitement. Dad helped him wheel the go-kart up to the starting line. Then, Jack hopped in, put on his helmet and got ready to race.

"Ready, steady, GO!" cried the starter. Jack whizzed off round the racetrack and before he knew it, he had overtaken a few of his friends.

Jack held on tight to the steering wheel and swerved around a big puddle. SPLOSH! One of the other go-karts drove straight into it, sending water splashing all over the track. "That was lucky," thought Jack.

Just then, he zoomed round a bend and straight into a tunnel. Switching on his torch headlights, Jack managed to race past even more of his friends in their go-karts.

As Jack hurtled towards the final stretch of the track, his heart was pounding. He was nearly in the lead! Then, Jack spotted an older boy called Dylan, up ahead. He had the best go-kart on the track. Just as Jack thought that Dylan was going to win, he remembered his horn. HONK! Dylan was so startled that he turned around, only to see Jack speeding up and passing him. ZOOM!

Jack hurtled across the finish line and the crowd roared and cheered. He had won the race in his very own, home-made go-kart!

Jack screeched to a stop. Then, he jumped out and gave Dad a big hug, as everyone crowded round to admire his winning go-kart. "My dad and I built it together," said Jack, proudly. "I can't wait to race it again next year."

Oliver's Birthday Treat

It was Oliver's birthday and Mum and Dad had promised him a special treat. Oliver raced downstairs to announce what he wanted. "I'm going to eat whatever I want, all day long," said Oliver, with a cheeky grin.

"If you're sure that's what you want," said Dad, smiling. First, Oliver wanted ice cream for breakfast. "I don't want just one scoop," said Oliver. "I want a whole mountain of ice cream, all to myself!"

So, Oliver took a big scoop of ice cream from every tub. Then, he squeezed gooey, sticky, strawberry sauce all over the top. "This is the perfect breakfast for a giant, ice cream ogre," thought Oliver, shovelling the ice cream into his mouth with the biggest spoon he could find. He finished the whole bowl and even polished off the melted ice cream at the bottom. SLURP!

Next, Oliver wanted some cookies, but he didn't want just one or two. "I want a whole castle of cookies!" said Oliver. His cookie castle had marshmallow towers and a chocolate milk moat. "This is perfect for a cookie king," he said. "If I got hungry, I could just nibble at the walls." It took a long time to build, but not long for Oliver to eat. MUNCH, CRUNCH!

Before Oliver knew it, it was time for lunch. "Let's have a picnic in the park," suggested Dad and he packed a huge basket of tasty sandwiches. When they got to the park, Oliver spotted a sweet stall. "I don't want sandwiches anymore," he said. "I want a whole stick of candy floss for lunch." Oliver gobbled up so much candy floss, his tongue turned pink!

Oliver had been having a wonderful time eating whatever he wanted, but by the end of the day, he was fed up of sweet treats. "What's for dinner, Mum?" asked Oliver, imagining something plain and not sugary at all.

"Well," began Mum, "as it's your special day, I thought we could have cake for dinner!" She came out of the kitchen carrying a huge birthday cake.

Oliver looked up at the cake, covered in gooey icing and sugary sprinkles. He felt very worried indeed and his tummy began to churn. GURGLE, GURGLE! He didn't think he could eat any more sweet things that day! Mum and Dad smiled at one another. "On second thought, let's save your cake until tomorrow and have a nice plate of spaghetti instead," said Mum. Oliver was relieved. "I think I've had enough treats for one day," he said.

The Marshmallow Monster

Eddie and his dad were having fun camping in the garden together. Dad was busy putting up their brand new, red tent and Eddie had run inside to get his comfy sleeping bag. When Eddie came back outside, Dad was sitting on the ground, looking very red indeed.

"What are you doing, Dad?" asked Eddie, with his little dog, Buster, trotting by his side. WOOF, WOOF!

"It's hard work putting up the tent!" puffed Dad. "Why don't we make a fire, instead? Then, I'll tell you a spooky story." Eddie loved scary tales and was always asking Dad to tell him his best ones.

"Yes, please!" cried Eddie. "I can't wait."

First, Dad and Eddie collected lots of sticks from around the garden.
Eddie made the tent nice and cosy, while Dad built the fire and soon,
it was flickering, popping and crackling. "Come on," said Dad. "I'll cook
the sausages and you can toast the marshmallows."
"Mmmm, these are delicious," said Eddie, popping a chewy
marshmallow in his mouth.

94

When their tummies were full and Eddie had finished the last toasted, gooey,
pink marshmallow, it was time for a spooky story.
"There once was a terrifying creature called the Marshmallow Monster,"
began Dad, lowering his voice. "It was pink and fluffy and gooey inside."
Eddie snuggled in his sleeping bag as Dad went on.

"The Marshmallow Monster wasn't unfriendly," whispered Dad, "but it was always hungry. It would sneak around campfires, looking for tasty treats to gobble up." Eddie pulled his sleeping bag up to his chin, as Dad went on. "One evening, a little boy was camping in the garden," said Dad. "He'd cooked some tasty sausages and scrumptious marshmallows on the fire. The Marshmallow Monster wanted nothing more than to have a taste."

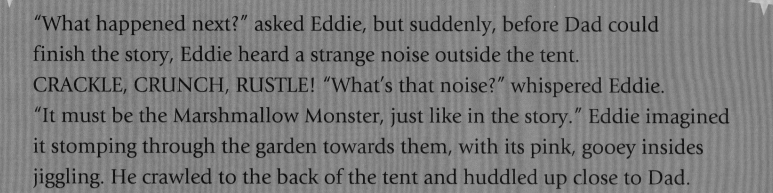

"What happened next?" asked Eddie, but suddenly, before Dad could finish the story, Eddie heard a strange noise outside the tent. CRACKLE, CRUNCH, RUSTLE! "What's that noise?" whispered Eddie. "It must be the Marshmallow Monster, just like in the story." Eddie imagined it stomping through the garden towards them, with its pink, gooey insides jiggling. He crawled to the back of the tent and huddled up close to Dad.

"Don't be scared," said Dad. "There's no such thing as monsters."
Dad grabbed the torch and shone it outside the tent. Eddie peeked out
from under his sleeping bag, as Dad started to laugh.

"What is it?" asked Eddie, nervously. "Has the Marshmallow Monster gone?"

"The only monster out here is Buster," said Dad, laughing. "He's been munching on the leftover sausages!" Eddie breathed a big sigh of relief.
"You gave me such a fright, Buster," said Eddie, as his little dog curled up next to him. "I'm glad you're not the Marshmallow Monster."
"I think you've had enough spooky stories for one night," said Dad.

99

Magic Marvin

Marvin had always wanted to be a magician, ever since he saw the Great Suprendo pull a real rabbit out of his hat. One day, Marvin decided to practise some tricks of his own. "I need to look just right to perform my magic," said Marvin. So, he put on his cape and picked up his wand.

Then, he put on his magician's hat and began to practise his tricks, but no matter how hard he tried, they all went terribly wrong.

"ABRACADABRA!" he cried, but he dropped his pack of cards all over the floor.

"ALACAZAM!" he shouted, but he dropped the coin which he'd tried to make disappear.

He even got his string of magic hankies tangled up, while his sister giggled in the hallway.

When there was a special announcement at school that there was going to be a big talent show, Marvin just knew he had to take part. "I'd love to perform my magic," he thought, "but what if everyone laughs at me?" Then, as Marvin was reading his superhero comics one night, he had a brilliant idea.

"I can wear a mask, just like a superhero," said Marvin. "Then, no one will know it's me if all my tricks go wrong." So, Marvin set to work. He cut out a cardboard mask and painted it gold. As soon as his disguise was ready, he practised his tricks until they were perfect.

103

When the night of the talent show finally arrived, Marvin's tummy felt like it was full of butterflies. He put on his mask and watched as his friends went on stage to sing, dance and tell jokes. The audience applauded loudly and by the time it was Marvin's turn, his hands were shaking so much that he could barely hold his wand.

Marvin took a deep breath and walked on stage. His first trick worked perfectly as he produced a bunch of flowers from his sleeve. The audience clapped and Marvin began to feel a bit better. Soon, he was making cards fly through the air and making his string of hankies disappear. "This mystery magician is much better than my brother," whispered Marvin's sister to her friends.

For his final trick, Marvin took off his top hat, waved his wand over it and said the magic words. Reaching into the hat, Marvin pulled out a white toy rabbit. The audience clapped and cheered and stamped their feet. "HURRAY, BRAVO!" they cried. Marvin was so pleased that his tricks had worked. "I don't need to hide behind this mask anymore," he thought.

So, Marvin took a bow and pulled off his mask and the audience's cheers grew louder and louder. After the show, Marvin's sister congratulated him.
"That was magic, Marvin," she said, kindly.
"That's a great name for a magician!" cried Marvin. "From now on, I'm going to call myself Magic Marvin."

Pirate Cove

Adam and his dad were visiting the Pirate Cove theme park. There were great pirate rides all around, but Adam couldn't wait for the famous pirate show. Suddenly, Adam heard a cannon in the distance. BOOM! "Come on, Dad," he said. "We've got to hurry, or we'll miss the start of the show."

Near the entrance to the show, Adam spotted two pirates talking and looking worried. "Pirate Pete is ill," said one, "and it's too late to find someone else. What are we going to do?" The other pirate shrugged and the parrot on his shoulder squawked, "No show, no show!"
Adam gasped. The show was the reason he'd come to Pirate Cove! Suddenly, he had a brilliant idea.

Adam felt really nervous, but he gathered up all his courage and went over to speak to the pirates. "Excuse me," he said, "I've always wanted to be a pirate. Can I be in the show instead of Pirate Pete?" The pirates looked at one other and smiled. "Follow us," they said, as they took Adam and his dad backstage.

The backstage dressing room was full of amazing props. There was a treasure chest full of jewels and gems and Adam even had his own costume. As he got dressed in his pirate hat, eyepatch and boots, Adam felt as though his tummy was full of butterflies. Suddenly, the pirate captain knocked on the door. "All aboard The Jolly Parrot!" he cried, leading Adam to the stage.

Adam heard a drum roll and as the pirates stepped aboard The Jolly Parrot, a sea shanty began to play. Adam felt even more nervous as the crowd clapped and cheered, but as soon as he stepped onto the stage, his nerves disappeared.

When the pirate captain called, "Count the buried treasure!" Adam opened the chest to find lots of gleaming, gold coins.

When the captain shouted "Anchors away!" Pirate Adam hoisted the pirate flag.

Then, the captain cried, "Scrub the deck!" When Adam missed a bit, the crew pretended to make him walk the plank.

Then, Adam climbed up to the crow's nest with Polly the parrot to be the ship's lookout. "I love being a pirate," thought Adam, as he peered through the telescope. "It's much more fun than being in the audience!" Suddenly, Adam heard a loud, slobbering, sucking noise. "What's that?" cried Adam.

He raced down to the deck and came face to face with a huge, purple creature that was covered in spots. It had big, scary eyes and long, wriggly tentacles. "Shiver me timbers!" cried Adam. He took out his pirate sword and cried, "Go back to the sea, ugly monster!" "You're too fierce for me, Pirate Adam," said the sea monster, slinking away from the ship.

"Well done, Pirate Adam!" cried the pirates, as the show came to an end.
"Land ahoy!" shouted Adam, then everyone danced a pirate jig. Even Polly
the parrot joined in and the audience clapped and cheered as Adam and the
pirates took a bow together.
"You make a brilliant pirate," said the crew. Adam felt really happy and he
couldn't wait for his next visit to Pirate Cove.

Treasure Hunt

It was Joe's birthday and he couldn't wait to open his presents. He burst into the living room and looked around for an enormous pile of gifts. There were bright balloons and a birthday banner, but there were no presents anywhere.

"Happy birthday," said Mum, handing Joe a piece of paper.
"What's this?" he asked. Joe looked at the paper, feeling very puzzled indeed.
"It's a clue for a special treasure hunt," explained Mum. "If you follow
the instructions, you'll find a wonderful surprise at the end."

117

Joe read out the first clue. *"Go and find the big machine, which makes our clothes all nice and clean,"* he read. "That's easy," said Joe, rushing into the kitchen. "It must be in the washing machine!" He went to look inside, but when he looked up, Joe found his second clue hidden on top, under the laundry basket.

"In this room you close your eyes, until the sun begins to rise," read Joe. "What does that mean?" asked Joe, scratching his head. He read it carefully a few more times and suddenly, the answer popped into his head. "I've got it!" he cried, running upstairs to his bedroom as fast as he could.

Joe searched all around his bedroom, looking for his next clue. He searched everywhere he could possibly think of, but still, he couldn't find it anywhere.

He looked under the bed, pushing toys and smelly socks out of the way.

He looked behind the dusty books on his shelves.

"It's not here," said Joe, sulking and sitting down on his bed. Just then, he spotted the third clue, poking out from under his pillow.

"You climb to the top, whoosh down and then stop," he read.

Joe thought as hard as he possibly could. He shut his eyes tight and concentrated, but his mind was blank. "I'll never find my birthday surprise," said Joe, sadly. Just then, as he was gazing out of his bedroom window, Joe spotted the answer to his clue. "The slide!" he shouted, racing downstairs.

Joe dashed outside to the garden and climbed up the steps of the slide. "WHEEEEEEEE!" he cried, as he whizzed down it. Suddenly, he noticed a gleaming, gold key at the bottom of the slide. Tied to the key was the final clue. Joe read it out, quietly.

"To find your treasure you must head inside the musty, dusty shed."

Joe darted over to the garden shed and unlocked the door with the little, gold key. CLICK! Inside, he found the coolest, shiniest, blue bike he had ever seen. It had a great big bow tied to it and Joe couldn't wait to go for a ride. "This is the best birthday present ever!" cried Joe.

The Bug Box

Max wanted a pet more than anything in the world. Whenever he asked for one, Mum always said no. So, one day, Max had a brilliant idea. "I know," he said to himself, "I'll just look in the garden and find a pet of my own." He found an empty box in the cupboard under the stairs and headed outside.

Max glanced all around the garden, where Dad was busy digging and Mum was hanging out the washing. "Where shall I look first?" he thought. Then, on the branch of an old tree, Max saw a beautiful spider's web. "You'll make a brilliant pet," he said, carefully placing the spider into the box.

When Dad had finished digging in the vegetable patch, Max decided to search there for a cool, new pet. "Dad is always complaining about caterpillars munching the lettuce," he thought. Sure enough, Max spotted a fat, wriggly caterpillar through his magnifying glass. "I can't wait to play with you," he said, as the caterpillar crawled into the box.

126

Next, Max went to look in the thick, tall grass behind the greenhouse. "I bet loads of interesting things live here," he said.

So, Max lay down on his tummy and soon, he spied a long line of busy ants, scurrying by. They marched like soldiers into Max's box to join the spider and the caterpillar.

Max searched outside, all afternoon. He'd never realised how many amazing things lived right there in his garden.

He found a friendly centipede under Mum's flowerpot...

... a shiny beetle in the shed...

... and he even found some insects, buzzing by the pond.

"I wonder how many bugs I've collected," thought Max, peering inside the box. By now, it had lots of wriggly, wiggly, slimy insects inside.

Soon, Max had run out of places to look. "All my new pets are so cool," said Max. "I can't wait to show Mum." As he dashed back inside to tell her the good news, Max smiled. "Mum will be so pleased," he thought. "Now, she doesn't have to buy me a pet at all."

Max burst into the kitchen. "Look, Mum!" he said, excitedly. "I have something much better than a puppy, a kitten, or a rabbit. I have lots of new pets, all of my own!" Mum turned around and before she knew it, Max had pulled the lid off of his bug box to show her what was inside. "AHHHHH!" screamed Mum.

"What's wrong, Mum?" said Max, looking worried.
"Mum doesn't like creepy crawlies," said Dad, laughing. Suddenly, Mum didn't think it would be so bad to have a nice, fluffy pet after all.
"Put them outside," said Mum, "and this time, we'll choose a pet together!"

Dan's Den

Dan and his friends really wanted a cool place to hang out in. They loved playing in Dan's bedroom, but his sister played her music so loudly, they could hear it through the wall. BOOM! BOOM! BOOM!

Liam held a pillow over his head and Callum put his hands over his ears.
"We can't stay here!" shouted Liam. "We need a proper den of our own."
"Let's go down to the garage," said Dan. "Maybe it will be quieter there."

When the boys looked in the garage, they gasped. There were tools and pots of spilt paint all over the floor and there wasn't much room with the car parked inside. "There are some chairs over there in the corner," suggested Callum, but Dan and Liam shook their heads.

"How about my sister's playhouse in the garden?" said Dan.

The boys trudged down the garden path and peered inside the playhouse. They had never seen so much pink in their whole lives! There were dollies and teddies everywhere and a little tea party was laid out on the table.

"We can't play in here," said Liam. "It's for girls!"

"We forgot about the shed," said Dan. "Follow me!"

Dan led Liam and Callum to the shed and flung the door open. It was packed with garden chairs, tools and flowerpots. It even had a leaky roof.
DRIP, DRIP, DRIP!
"We'll get mouldy if we stay in here," said Dan. "There's only one way we're going to get our very own den. We'll have to build one!"

Liam and Callum nodded in excitement. "That's a great idea!" cried Liam. "Let's get started," said Callum. First, Dan asked Mum if they could borrow the clothes-drying rack. Then, the others collected as many old, spare blankets and pillows as they could. "I know," said Callum, when the den was nearly finished. "Let's make a tunnel for the entrance!"

While Callum and Liam built the tunnel, Dan raced upstairs to find his comics. Soon, the boys had a proper den all to themselves and they couldn't wait to play in it. They spent the whole afternoon in the den, telling stories and jokes. They made even more noise than Dan's sister!

138

Then, they ate delicious cupcakes and sipped fizzy drinks and soon, it was time for Liam and Callum to go home. "That was the best afternoon, ever," said Dan. "I can't wait to hang out in our den tomorrow. There's no den as good as the one you make yourself."

The Dog Detective

Archie had always wanted a puppy, so he couldn't wait to bring home Scruff from the pet rescue centre.

"Scruff is going to be the best pet, ever," said Archie.

Scruff wagged his tail and sniffed with his shiny, wet nose.

"I'm sure he'll get settled in no time," said Mum, as Archie carried Scruff inside.

Scruff, however, did not settle at all. In fact, he was always in trouble. Each day, he did something even more naughty than the day before.

"Scruff, no!" cried Archie, as Scruff leapt onto the sofa. He tore open the cushions so all the stuffing came out.

"Stop, Scruff!" Archie cried, as Scruff ran through the kitchen, leaving muddy paw prints everywhere.

"Naughty, Scruff!" yelled Archie. "Look what you've done to my best sweater."

Scruff got up to all sorts of mischief. Then, one day, Mum was searching for a missing sock. Scruff raced into her bedroom looking for someone to play with and darted all over the room, until she nearly tripped over him. "Scruff, go outside!" she shouted. When Mum came back downstairs, she found Scruff waiting at the back door. He had something purple and fluffy in his mouth. "It's my missing sock!" cried Mum.

Soon, Dad was missing something, too. "Has anybody seen my tie?" he asked, peering behind the chair and under the table. Straight away, Scruff's ears pricked up. He scampered out of the room and moments later, he was back. "My tie!" cried Dad, as Scruff, dropped the stripy tie at his feet. "Good boy, Scruff," said Dad, patting him on the head.

Scruff found Archie's homework under the bed and Mum's gloves behind the sofa. He even managed to sniff out where Dad had put the garage key. Before they knew it, Scruff was helping Archie's whole family to find their missing things and he wasn't causing any trouble at all.

"Scruff isn't naughty at all," said Mum. "He just needs something to do. Being a dog detective seems like the perfect role in this family."
"We're always losing things," said Archie, grinning. "I'm sure we'll have plenty of cases for Scruff to solve!"

145

Robbie's Robot

Robbie had always wanted a robot. "I'd like a big, red one that beeps and has lots of flashing lights," he said. "It could even do my homework and tidy my room!" So, one day, Robbie decided to build a robot of his own. He gathered together everything he needed and set to work.

Robbie worked hard all day and by bedtime, his eyelids began to feel heavy. "I'll have to finish my robot tomorrow," he said, yawning. He snuggled down under his duvet and drifted off into a lovely, deep sleep. Suddenly, Robbie sat up in bed. He thought he could hear a strange, beeping sound in the darkness. BEEP, BEEP, BEEP!

Robbie opened his eyes to see his robot moving slowly across the desk, with its eyes flashing. "My robot has come to life," gasped Robbie, leaping out of bed. He decided to give the robot an order. "Tidy my room," he commanded. At once, the robot began to push all of Robbie's books and toys into a neat pile.

Robbie smiled. "It's tidying my room for me, just like I always wanted," he whispered. Just as the robot finished putting away the last toy, there was a strange, clunking noise that sounded like grinding metal. The robot stopped tidying and started flinging things across Robbie's bedroom.
"Stop!"cried Robbie.

"Maybe the robot will be better at doing my homework," thought Robbie. "Work out these sums," he ordered. Immediately, the robot picked up a pencil and began writing the answers in Robbie's maths book. It was finishing the very last question when Robbie heard the same clunking, grinding noise the robot had made before.

Suddenly, the robot began tearing his maths book into tiny pieces.
RIP, RIP, RIP! "Oh, no," groaned Robbie. "Stop, you silly robot!" he shouted.
The robot didn't stop and Robbie's room became messier and messier.
The clunking noise was so loud that Robbie hid under his duvet to try and
block it out.

The robot kept beeping and Robbie could hear it coming closer and closer towards him. BEEP! BEEP! BEEP! "I wish I'd never built a robot," he thought. "It's all gone horribly wrong!" BEEP! BEEP! BEEP! Robbie opened his eyes and peeped out from under the duvet. He realised that the noise wasn't coming from his robot at all. It was just his alarm clock. "Phew!" said Robbie. "It was all just a dream."

Robbie looked around his bedroom and saw that it was just as he'd left it the night before. His maths book was still in one piece and his toys were exactly where he'd left them. The robot was still half-finished. "I think I'll be better off tidying my room and doing my homework by myself," said Robbie, picking up the robot and putting it away for another day, "at least for now!" he said, with a cheeky grin.

I'm Not Scared

It was a beautiful, sunny day and Michael and his little brother, Timmy, were playing at the park. Even though Timmy was younger, he loved to go on the exciting rides. "Look at me!" cried Timmy, swinging up high on the swings. "WHEEEEE!"

"I don't like swinging up high," said Michael, looking up at Timmy.

"Michael's a scaredy-cat!" cried Timmy. "He's too scared to swing high, like me."

"Michael doesn't have to swing high if he doesn't want to, Timmy," said Mum.

"Why don't you both have a go on another ride?" she suggested.

So, Michael and Timmy went to play on the roundabout. Michael held on tightly as Timmy pushed him round and round. "Don't go so fast!" cried Michael, but Timmy didn't stop.

"You're a scaredy-cat!" called Timmy, still pushing as fast as he could, while Michael gripped onto the bars.

Next, they spotted the see-saw. Timmy plonked down onto the seat straight away, but Michael sat down, nervously. Timmy pushed off the ground with his feet and his end of the see-saw shot up. "WHOOPEE!" cried Timmy. Then, he came down to the ground with a BUMP and Michael's end of the see-saw whooshed upwards. "AHHHH!" yelled Michael.

Finally, Michael and Timmy headed over to the slide. Michael went up first, climbing step by step. "Hurry up!" called Timmy, eagerly, from below. Michael sat at the top of the slide and held on, too afraid to let go. "You're a scaredy-cat," said Timmy, as Michael finally let go and whooshed down the slide with his eyes shut tight.

"You're no fun to play with," said Timmy. "'I'm going to play football with those boys, instead."

"No, don't!" cried Michael. "You're too small to play with them." Timmy didn't listen. He ran over to the boys who were running around and kicking a ball. Timmy was soon in the middle of the group of boys, but he suddenly began to feel worried.

Michael saw his little brother looking nervous and suddenly, he didn't feel scared anymore. "Please don't play so close to my little brother," said Michael. "He's smaller than you and he might get hurt." "Sorry," said the boys, picking up their ball and running to play on the other side of the park. Timmy looked at Michael and thought how brave he was. "I'll never call you a scaredy-cat again," said Timmy, as they walked back to the swings together.